Learn with Peppa Pig

Mr Bull's New Teapot

Adapted by
Laura Baker

Learn Phonics with Peppa Pig

Phonics teaches children to read by learning the sounds of a language. They start by learning the sound for each letter or combination of letters, which helps them to break down words into sounds (**th-i-nk**). They can then blend these sounds together to read whole words ("think"). This is called sounding out and blending.

As children learn more sounds, they will meet them in lots of different combinations. With practice, they will learn to sound out and blend the sounds together to read new words.

Listen carefully as your child reads the **Learn with Peppa** stories with you. Encourage them to sound out and blend each word. If they find a word difficult, help them to sound it out. Most importantly, have fun!

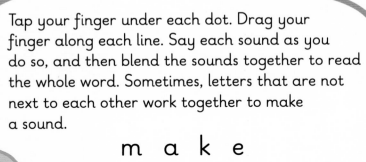

Tap your finger under each dot. Drag your finger along each line. Say each sound as you do so, and then blend the sounds together to read the whole word. Sometimes, letters that are not next to each other work together to make a sound.

m a k e

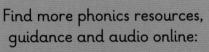

Find more phonics resources, guidance and audio online:

www.learnwithpeppa.com

Mr Bull's New Teapot

Read the sounds
Practise sounding out and blending to read these words.

a m a z e d

b r o k e n

ch i n a

e v e n i n g

h o le

j i g s aw

n ew s p a p er

sh r ie k e d

s m i le d

Practise the words
These words cannot be sounded out in this way. Read them with your child.

all	by	could	Mr	my
myself	of	oh	said	some
somehow	they	was	were	when
would	your			

Meet the friends
These names are not as easy to sound out and blend! Read them with your child.

Daddy Pig   George   Mr Bull   Mummy Pig

Mummy and Daddy Pig were out shopping with Peppa Pig and George when they saw Mr Bull.

Mr Bull's crew were digging a hole in the road outside Miss Rabbit's china shop.

Miss Rabbit came out and shrieked, "Stop!"

Smash! Crash! Dig!

Miss Rabbit's shop was full of elegant items that could crack and smash.

Your digging has shaken all my china!

Mr Bull saw the teapot in Miss Rabbit's hands.
He threw his tools aside and took it from her.

Mr Bull went inside. He said, "In the evening, I like to brew a strong cup of tea as I read my newspaper. I will treat myself to a new teapot."

By the time he reached the till, the teapot was broken! Mr Bull was too strong.

"Oh no!" cried Miss Rabbit. "That's a shame."

Then Miss Rabbit saw how upset Mr Bull was.

"Hand it over. I can help you," she said.

The teapot was like a jigsaw, but Miss Rabbit completed it with some glue.

"Good as new," she said.

Hooray!

Peppa and George did not think the teapot could be fixed. They were amazed.

Mr Bull shouted, too. "HOORAY!"

"Good grief!" said Miss Rabbit. "You could smash it, Mr Bull."

Mr Bull said, "Oops. I will turn my inside volume down!"

They all rode back with Mr Bull to test his new teapot.

They chugged along at a crawl to keep it safe.

They made it back to Mr Bull's tent. Somehow, the teapot was unbroken! They all smiled.

Mr Bull gave Peppa, George, Mummy and Daddy Pig and all the crew some tea. He set the teapot down . . .

Smash!

Mr Bull groaned.

Oh dear. Now they would have to go back to Miss Rabbit's shop!

Have fun with Peppa Pig

 A   Answer these questions about the story.

1 What was Mr Bull's crew doing outside Miss Rabbit's china shop?

2 When did Mr Bull like to read his newspaper?

3 How did Miss Rabbit fix the broken teapot?

4 Where was Mr Bull when he broke the teapot for a second time?

5 Read page 18 again. Which word tells us that the teapot is still in one piece?

B

Can you speak like Mr Bull? Try saying "I will treat myself to a new teapot!" in Mr Bull's loud voice!

Tell me a story

You can be a storyteller! Make up a new story that starts with what you can see in this picture.

C

Have you ever broken something?
Were you able to fix it?
What happened?

LADYBIRD BOOKS
UK | USA | Canada | Ireland | Australia | India | New Zealand | South Africa
Ladybird Books is part of the Penguin Random House group of companies
whose addresses can be found at global.penguinrandomhouse.com.
www.penguin.co.uk   www.puffin.co.uk   www.ladybird.co.uk

Adapted from:
Peppa Pig: Mr Bull in a China Shop first published by Ladybird Books Ltd 2014
Learn with Peppa Pig edition published by Ladybird Books Ltd 2023
001
© 2023 ABD Ltd/Ent. One UK Ltd/Hasbro

Adapted by Laura Baker
Phonics consultant: Charlotte Raby

Licensed by

Printed in China

The authorized representative in the EEA is Penguin Random House Ireland,
Morrison Chambers, 32 Nassau Street, Dublin D02 YH68

A CIP catalogue record for this book is available from the British Library

ISBN: 978-0-241-57649-6

All correspondence to:
Ladybird Books, Penguin Random House Children's
One Embassy Gardens, 8 Viaduct Gardens, London SW11 7BW

MIX
Paper from
responsible sources
FSC® C018179

FSC
www.fsc.org

Created and developed especially for pre-schoolers,
Learn with Peppa features a dedicated app and a fantastic range of books
to support your little ones on their early learning adventures!

www.learnwithpeppa.com